For the real Ellie – and for Ellie's mum – AD
For Nicholas with lots of love – KM

## Crabtree Publishing Company
www.crabtreebooks.com

PMB 16A, 350 Fifth Avenue,
Suite 3308,
New York, NY
10118

612 Welland Avenue,
St. Catharines,
Ontario, Canada
L2M 5V6

Published by Crabtree Publishing Company in 2004
Published in 2002 by Random House Children's Books and Red Fox

Cataloging-in-Publication data

Durant, Alan.
    That's not right! / written by Alan Durant ; illustrated by Katherine McEwen.
        p. cm. – (Flying foxes)
    Summary: Squashing a bug isn't as straightforward as it seems, especially when it is seen from the bug's perspective!
    ISBN 0-7787-1486-1 (RLB) – ISBN 0-7787-1532-9 (PB)
    [1. Nature–Fiction. 2. Conflict management–Fiction.] I. McEwen, Katherine  ill. II. Title. III. Series.
                        2003022722
                        LC

Text copyright © Alan Durant 2002
Illustrations copyright © Katharine McEwen 2002

The right of Alan Durant and Katharine McEwen to be identified as the author and illustrator of this work has been asserted in accordance with the Copyright, Designs and Patents Act, 1988.

Set in Cheltenham Book Infant

1 2 3 4 5 6 7 8 9 0  Printed and bound in Malaysia by Tien Wah Press  0 9 8 7 6 5 4 3

# t's Not Right!

Alan Durant
Katharine McEwen

Ellie's class was writing stories
about animals.

5

Ellie chose a bug.
This is what Ellie wrote:

# Ellie's Story

Once there was a bug. His name was Fred. He lived under a stone.

One day Fred came out. A big shoe stamped down and squashed him.

# Splat!

Fred was dead.
The end.

Ellie read the story to her teacher.

"What a sad story!" the teacher said.
"It has a beginning, a middle, and an end,"
said Ellie.
"So it does," her teacher agreed.

Ellie read the story to her brother.
"That's a funny story," he laughed.

Ellie read the story to her mom.

"What a strange story, Ellie," said her mom.

"It has a beginning, a middle, and an end," said Ellie proudly.

Her mom smiled. "Very good, Ellie," she said.

That evening, the moon was full and bright. It was like a giant eye. Ellie sat on the front step to look at it. The moon winked at her.

Something moved on the path in front of Ellie. "Excuse me," said a tiny voice, "but that's not right!"

Ellie looked down and saw a sow bug.

"I am not really a bug," hissed the sow bug. His antennae waggled crossly. "A bug is a kind of insect. Insects have six legs. I have seven pairs of legs. I am a crustacean, if you must know, like a lobster or a crab."

"Oh," said Ellie. "You don't look like a crab."

"Perhaps not," agreed the sow bug, "but I do have a hard shell-like body. Lift me up and see."

Ellie put her hand on the ground and the sow bug crawled onto it. She gazed at the sow bug. Its body looked a bit like gray armor.

"I see what you mean," she said.

The sow bug tapped his antennae against her hand. "Now, listen," he said. "I'll tell *you* the story."

# Fred's Story

There was once a handsome sow bug called Fred.

He had the finest antennae you ever did see. He lived under a large, cool stone in the garden. His home was dark and damp and lovely. One day Fred was hungry. He crawled out of his house to look for food.

19

Suddenly, a big, bully shoe stamped
down and tried to squash him. But
Fred was too clever and too quick.
He curled up in a ball and rolled away.
Then he crawled back under his
cool stone and lived happily
ever after.
The end.

"I like that story," said Ellie.
"There's nothing like a happy ending,"
purred Fred.

Something else moved in the bush beside Ellie.

"That's not right!" a little voice hissed. It was another sow bug.

"Hello," said Ellie. "Who are you?"

"I'm Mrs. Fred," said the sow bug. "I'm Fred's wife." She waggled her antennae.

"That story just won't do at all," she snorted. "A good story needs more than one character. How could my dear darling Freddy live happily ever after without someone to love?"

"Someone like you?" said Ellie.

"That's right," said Mrs. Fred. "Now, dearie, you listen to me."

# Mrs. Fred's Story

Once upon a time and not so very far away, there lived a lovely sow bug named Fred. Oh, he was handsome. His antennae were as fine as fine could be. But Fred was not happy. He was all alone in the world. "If only I had someone to love," he said sadly to himself.

Well, one day Fred came out from under his stone to look for food, and what did he spy? Why, a beautiful lady sow bug!

It was love at first sight. Fred crawled toward her. But then, oh, something terrible happened!

A monster shoe appeared. It stamped down and tried to squash poor Fred.

"Look out!" cried the beautiful lady sow bug.

Now, luckily, Fred was clever and Fred was quick. In a flash, he curled up in a ball and rolled away.

# Wham!
# Bam!

The shoe stamped
down on the stone. Ow!
The stone was sharp and
cut the shoe. The shoe
limped away.

Fred scuttled to his love. "Will you marry
me?" he asked.
"Of course, my darling," said the
beautiful lady sow bug.
They got married right away and lived
happily ever after. The end.

"It's true," sighed Fred. "It was love at first sight."

Fred and Mrs. Fred rubbed antennae.

"What a lovely story," said Ellie. "It is very romantic."

# Stamp, stamp!

**"That's not right!"** cried an angry voice. **"That story is garbage!"**

Ellie looked around and frowned. "Who said that?" she asked.

**"I did!"** said an old blue shoe lying on the path. It looked grumpy, as if its laces were in a knot. **"I'm not a bully or a monster. Why should I be the bad one in the story? It's not fair."**

"No one cares about my feelings."

31

"You should see things from my point of view," said the shoe. "How would you like to be cut by a sharp stone?"

"Well, I wouldn't," said Ellie. "But I wouldn't like to be squashed flat either."

"That's right," agreed Fred and Mrs. Fred.

"It's not my fault. It's the person who wears me who's to blame," argued the shoe.

"Anyway, who cares about creepy crawlies? They're all pests." He stuck out his tongue at Fred and Mrs. Fred.

"Not true!" cried Mrs. Fred. "We are not pests! We are good for the garden."

"Yes," Fred added. "We eat dead plants and vegetable peels. Then they come out the other end in our poo and feed the soil, which helps new plants grow."

"That's right, dear," Mrs. Fred agreed proudly. "People recycle bottles and cans; we recycle nature."

"I didn't know that," said Ellie. "That is good."

**"Hmm."** The shoe shuffled impatiently.

"Why don't you tell us your story?" said Ellie.

**"About time too,"** said the shoe.

# The Shoe's Story

One day, a big, blue, beautiful, shiny new shoe was walking in the garden. He had just been given a new pair of striped laces and he was feeling very happy. Suddenly, a *silly* sow bug came out, *without looking*, right in front of him. The shoe tried to pull back, but it was too late.

Down he went.

The sow bug curled into a ball and rolled away. The shoe landed on a sharp stone.

"Ow!" shrieked the shoe. He was badly hurt. The sow bug got away without a scratch, but the poor, brave shoe had a big cut and a lot of scuffs. He had to go to the cobbler to be mended. But he was never the same again and his fine striped laces were given to another pair of shoes. The end.

"That is a sad story," said Ellie.

"I think the shoe got just what he deserved," said Fred.

"I agree, dear," said Mrs. Fred. "Big bully." And with that, the two sow bugs disappeared.

**"Insects!"** tutted the shoe.

"They're not insects," Ellie corrected him. "They're a kind of crustacean – like crabs."

"Oh, really!" huffed the shoe and that was his last word.

The full moon winked again.

"Supper time, Ellie!" called Ellie's mom.

That evening, before bed, Ellie wrote a new story.

"A talking sow bug!" said her brother.

"A grumpy bully shoe!" said her mom.

"What a crazy story!" they cried.

"But it's true!" said Ellie.

The end.

That's not right!

Put on Ellie's storyteller shoes.

The moon

Listen to how each of the characters in Ellie's tale tells the story. How is each one's version different? Look at how the characters are pictured. Did you notice how they don't always look the same – why?

Fred

Mrs. Fred

Can you tell the story from the moon's point of view? What kind of character do you think the moon might be? Helpful, wise, boastful?

Be a storyteller like me!

The shoe

Tell a friend about what you did at recess today. Now pretend you are an ant or the slide in the playground and tell the same story. How would it sound?

Ellie

## Make a sow bug home and observe.

Find us in damp, dark places.

Find a sow bug under a stone or log outside.

Place about one inch (2.5 cm) of damp soil in an empty shoe box. Put a piece of wood on top of the soil. Add some twigs and dead leaves. Next, put your sow bug inside.

Make small holes in the lid of the box.

Spray the soil with water and cover.

Check your sow bug home every day. Spray it with water, but don't make it too wet! After a few days, return your sow bug to nature.

Sow bug poo makes good plant food.

Does your sow bug like light or shade? What does it eat? Watch it walk!

45

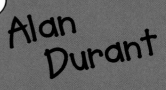

# Alan Durant

**Where did you get the idea for this story?** One evening my daughter asked me for a story. I was tired so I told her a very short story about a hedgehog that got squashed by a car. "That's not right!" she said, and she told the story back to me with a different twist. A squashed hedgehog didn't seem very nice, so I changed the main character to a sow bug instead.

**Which character in this story are you most like and why?** I am like the moon because the way it looks down over everything, watching it happen, is a bit like being an author. Mind you, some people would probably say I'm more like the grumpy shoe!

**What do you do if you get stuck on your writing?** I jump up and down and stamp my feet (so maybe I am like the shoe). Then I write something else until I'm not stuck any more.

**What did you like to do when you were a child? What did you hate most?** I liked anything to do with football plus reading, singing, making up stories, and dressing up. I hated eating applesauce, going to the dentist, and getting up early, and I still hate all those things!

# Katharine McEwen

Katharine as a child

**How did you paint the pictures in this book?**
First, I drew out the pictures.
Next, I painted them using
watercolors and then drew over
the top of them with pencil crayons.
It took me about a month from start to finish.

**Which character in the story did you most like to draw and why?** I liked drawing the sow bug best, because I enjoyed the challenge of getting it to look like a human character that talks.

**Which character do you wish you could be like?** I wish I could be like Ellie and make up stories as easily as she does.

**What's your favorite place to draw?** I like to work in my studio with a nice big cup of tea and a bag of chocolate cookies!

**Did you draw when you were a child?**
I used to draw all the time, as you
can see from the photo of me
above, aged two!

Will you try and write or draw a story too?

*Let your ideas take flight with*

# Flying Foxes

### Digging for Dinosaurs
by Judy Waite and Garry Parsons

### Only Tadpoles Have Tails
by Jane Clarke and Jane Gray

### The Magic Backpack
by Julia Jarman and Adriano Gon

### Slow Magic
by Pippa Goodhart and John Kelly

### Sherman Swaps Shells
by Jane Clarke and Ant Parker

### That's Not Right!
by Alan Durant and Katharine McEwen

"I heard your story," said the sow bug, "and I didn't like it."

"Oh," said Ellie. "What was wrong?"

"It wasn't very nice," said the sow bug. "Some of my best friends are bugs."

"Oh, I'm sorry," said Ellie. "I didn't mean to upset you."

"What kind of bug was it anyway?" asked the sow bug.

"One like you," said Ellie, "A sow bug."